AND THE MUMMY'S CURSE

PaRRagon

Bath · New York · Singapore · Hong Kong · Cologne · Delhi · Melbourne

Written by Zed Storm
Creative concept and words by E. Hawken
Check out the website at www.will-solvit.com

First edition published by Parragon in 2010

Parragon
Queen Street House
4 Queen Street
Bath BA1 1HE, UK

ISBN 978-1-4075-8979-4

Printed in China

Please retain this information for future reference.

CONTENTS

Awesome!

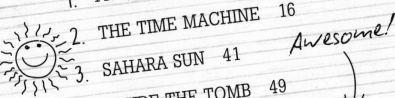

?

?

I sang at the top of my lungs as I ran down the school corridor, throwing stink bombs as I went. "One more day to go, one more day of sorrow, one more day of this old dump, and I'll be home tomorrow!"

"Will Solvit! Get back here this minute."

That sounded a lot like my teacher – Mrs Simmons. I hadn't meant her to hear me or see me for that matter. I was going to be in BIG trouble.

"If it wasn't the last day of school I'd be putting you in detention," she said. "Get in the classroom now!" Her face turned super-red – kind of like a baboon's backside.

I did as I was told and headed for the

7   he he!

classroom, sitting down next to my best friend, Zoe. She has helped me out on many of my past adventures – when I was fighting a bunch of alien cats called the Partek and then with the rehoming of my pet dinosaur, Rex. You think that sounds crazy? Well, perhaps it's time to tell you a bit about myself.

I'm called Will Solvit. I'm ten years old and I'm an Adventurer. All my family have been Adventurers before me, even my Grandpa Monty who I live with right now. My dad is one too. He's stuck in a dinosaur-infested jungle at the moment with my mum – although that's another story altogether.

That's enough about me for now. Zoe was nudging me to keep quiet as Mrs Simmons had come into the classroom and had started talking.

"Since it's the last day of school," she said,

"it's time to present your projects to the class. I hope you've all come prepared."

My brain scrambled to remember... That's it – everyone had to write a project about their favourite ancient Egyptian thing and, of course, I hadn't done it.

I did know a few things about the ancient Egyptians that are pretty cool though: *Cool!*

- They used to pull people's brains out through their nose with a hook before they made them into mummies.
- They had pet monkeys.
- They wrote in pictures, called hieroglyphs, instead of words.

There are also loads of things the ancient Egyptians used to do that aren't so cool. Did you know they used to grind up old mummy bones and put them into potions that they drank?

Urrrrrrrrrgh!

Anyway, just as one of the boys in my class started to present his project, I felt my SurfM8 50 (it's a kind of internet phone) buzzing in my pocket. Quietly, I took it out and read the IM message. It was from Zoe (her IM name is SingaporeSista). It went something like this:

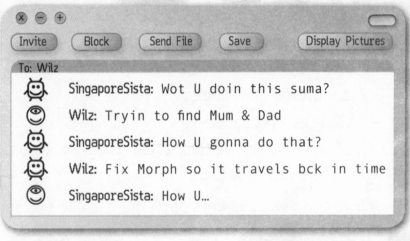

Invite   Block   Send File   Save   Display Pictures

To: Wilz

SingaporeSista: Wot U doin this suma?

Wilz: Tryin to find Mum & Dad

SingaporeSista: How U gonna do that?

Wilz: Fix Morph so it travels bck in time

SingaporeSista: How U...

But I didn't get to read the rest of Zoe's message because suddenly Mrs Simmons was

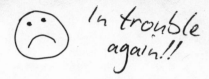
In trouble again!!

howling like a starving hyena. Then, in a
well-practised move, she snatched my SurfM8.
It disappeared like a flash into her 'confiscated'
drawer which she locked tight with the firm twist
of a key.

I was well and truly busted. How was I meant
to IM Zoe without a SurfM8?

But now Mrs Simmons was talking again, or
rather wailing like a screeching cat. "Since you
know so much about the Egyptians that you don't
have to listen in class, Will, you can present your
project next!"

Uh oh. I was going to have to think super-fast
to get out of this one.

"Um, er... um... well, sorry, Mrs Simmons,"
I said. "I put my project in a safe and then lost
the combination."

"If you think I'll believe that, I'll believe

anything," she said, sounding annoyed.

"Oh yes, well, er, maybe now I think about it," I said quickly, "I think I put the project on my windowsill and an eagle flew down and took it away to build a nest."

At this point everyone in the class started laughing.

"Enough, Will," said my teacher, looking like smoke was about to start pouring out of her nose. "Just tell me where your project is."

I thought fast – which hopeless excuse could I try next?

I wrote it in invisible ink?

I'm allergic to paper?

"Er...er..."

"ENOUGH!" Mrs Simmons bellowed. "You clearly haven't done it, so over the summer you can write a project three times as long as anyone else's. Then instead of presenting it to the class, you can present it to the entire school!"

Uh oh! There was no way I was cheering when the school bell rang. The whole summer holidays spent writing a project? How dumb had I been? Feeling pretty gutted, I left the classroom with Zoe skipping beside me.

"Cheer up, Will," she chirped. "We've broken up!"

"Yeah, and I have to spend the holidays writing about people that have been dead for thousands of years," I groaned. "If only I had done my project when I was meant to."

"C'mon," Zoe smiled, "bet you can't run home faster than me."

"You're on," I laughed, momentarily putting what I'd done, or hadn't done, behind me.

I didn't even have time to draw breath as Zoe

was already bolting away towards the school gates and freedom.

Quickly, I ran after her and we raced all the way back to Grandpa Monty's house, stopping only on the driveway to catch our breath.

"Who are all these statues, anyway?" Zoe asked, pointing to the dozens of old people lining the mile-long driveway that were covered in moss and bird poo. Some of them were so ancient, you couldn't even read the names carved into the bottom of them.

"They're my ancestors," I answered.

We walked past the statues and read the names on the ones we could see:

GRACE SOLVIT
1750 - 1811
ARTIST

GEORGE SOLVIT
1919 - 2000
EGYPTOLOGIST

SEBASTIAN
SOLVIT
1719 - 1786
ASTRONOMER

"They were all Adventurers," I was explaining to Zoe when suddenly she shrieked.

"Will! Look!"

I could see exactly why Zoe was excited.

There was something sitting next to the statue of George Solvit – a letter. A letter with my name on it. And, from past experience, I knew exactly what that meant – an Adventure was about to begin.

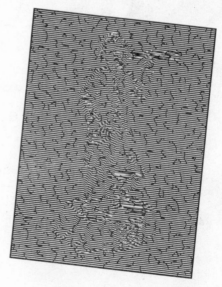

CHAPTER TWO
THE TIME MACHINE

How did the boy get Egyptian flu?
He caught it from his mummy!

An adventure is about to begin.

To know where to start, you need the help of
one of your long-dead ancestors.
Study your family tree.

"That's not much of a clue as to where to start,"
Zoe said as I folded up the letter and put it in my
school bag.

"I'll figure it out," I said confidently. If I was
honest, I had no idea where to begin, but I didn't
want to tell Zoe that. I was quiet as we walked up

the driveway. Solvit Hall loomed over us as we headed to the front door.

The mansion's been in my family for generations, and is nearly as ancient as a dinosaur. Grandpa Monty lives there now. It's pretty creepy and looks like the kind of place a vampire might live with over a hundred windows and turrets that stretch into the sky – even a family of bats lives in the roof. Apparently there are secret passages in the house, but I'm not so sure – I haven't found any yet.

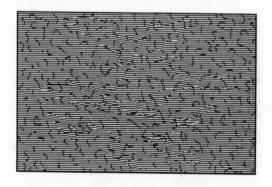

We were about seven statues from the front door when Grandpa's terrier, Plato, bounded towards us. He leapt into the air, yapping happily.

"Hey, Zoe," I said, ruffling Plato's messy fur. "Why do dogs wag their tails? Because no one else will do it for them!"

Zoe shook her head and chuckled as we headed inside to the kitchen. Grandpa Monty was sitting at the table, reading the paper and eating some weird-looking concoction.

"Fish heads and lizards' tails soup in case you're wondering," Grandpa said with a smile, pointing to his bowl. "You two like some?"

GROSS!

"Er, not today thanks, Grandpa," I said as politely as I could. Grandpa Monty is as crazy as a kangaroo in an Easter bunny costume. "Any cake going instead?" I asked.

"Is Jessica staying for tea?" Grandpa asked, totally ignoring me.

"I'm Zoe," Zoe reminded him. (Grandpa's useless with names.) "And yes, please."

Grandpa slurped down the rest of his soup and put the bowl on the floor for Plato to lick clean.

"Make yourselves comfortable then," Grandpa Monty smiled. "Two dinners fit for a Pharaoh coming right up!"

Zoe and I sat at the kitchen table while Grandpa clunked pots and pans about. We talked for ages about what the letter could mean.

"How is an ancestor meant to help me when they're dead?" I wondered aloud.

"I wish I could help but I'm off to Singapore tomorrow to see my dad," Zoe said apologetically.

"That's OK," I replied, although I didn't feel OK about it at all. I didn't mind having Zoe around any more and I liked being able to talk to someone else about being an Adventurer.

Grandpa placed a steaming mound of food on the table in front of us. "Peanut butter soufflé!" he said proudly.

Peanut butter soufflé might sound weird, but it's actually quite tasty. Zoe and I gobbled it down with jelly and ice-cream-coated carrots while Plato sat at our feet and looked at us longingly. I tossed him a couple of carrots to keep him happy.

Zoe's mum came to pick her up after dinner.

"I'll IM and call you all summer," Zoe told me as I waved her off outside the house.

"Thanks!" I shouted back, feeling surprisingly

sad as the car drove away. Shoulders slumped, I headed back into the house and up the stairs towards my bedroom.

My Grandpa's driver, Stanley, was on the landing, polishing pictures of my ancestors. He said hello to me and I smiled back. Stanley knows the US President and helped warn him about the Partek when they tried to invade Earth!

I walked on down the corridor to my room. School was over, which was great. But my only friend had gone away for the summer and I had no idea how to get my next Adventure under way.

Quickly, I walked over to my Morphing Anatomical Dark Energy Device (Morph for short). Morph is Dad's greatest-ever invention. It can turn into whatever you want it to be, and once you've finished using it, it shrinks back down to a miniature version of what you last used it for. This time I turned it into a computer and typed the word 'ancestor' into the search engine. This is what came up:

A person from whom one is descended.

Then I typed in the words 'family tree' and this came up:

A chart showing the ancestry, descent and relationship of all members of a family.

That was no help. So I typed in 'family' and then 'tree' separately:

A group consisting of parents and children.

A plant with a woody main stem or trunk, studied by botanists.

One of my ancestors was a botanist – that was their special skill. Was my botanist ancestor the one who was meant to help me?

I rushed out of my room, back to the staircase and looked at the plaques next to the portraits at the top of the stairs.

CAROLINE SOLVIT
1801 - 1896
DEEP-SEA DIVER

CAPTAIN LUKE SOLVIT
1777 - 1850
FLEET COMMANDER

CLIFFORD SOLVIT
1832 - 1926
EXPLORER

Then I saw this one:

HENRIETTA SOLVIT
1835 - 1900
BOTANIST

But as I looked at her picture, I couldn't work out quite how Henrietta was meant to help me.

- Did I have to visit her grave and dig up her bones?
- Did she keep some kind of diary hidden in Solvit Hall that I had to find?
- Did she discover a special plant with magical powers? Was I meant to become a botanist too?

"What are you up to, Will?" Stanley asked.

"Trying to figure out how a long-dead relative can help me," I replied. "Can you do me a favour?"

"Of course."

"Please can you take this picture off the wall?"
I pointed to the portrait of Henrietta. "There's
something I need to check out."

Carefully, Stanley lifted the portrait down and
carried it up the stairs to the landing before
placing it on the floor.

"I'm not sure how a picture's going to help,"
I muttered.

Stanley shook his head and smiled, "Don't
judge everything by appearances. It's what's
inside that really counts."

What on earth did Stanley mean? What could be
inside a picture?

Carefully, I turned the portrait upside down and
ran my fingers over the canvas seam at the back.

"Do you have a knife I can borrow?" I asked.

"Allow me," Stanley said.

Taking a sharp flick-blade out of his pocket, he

ran it along the seam of the painting before lifting off the back of the portrait. Inside was an envelope with my name on it.

Success!

I ripped open the envelope right there; I didn't care that Stanley was watching.

There wasn't just a letter inside the envelope; there was a computer chip!

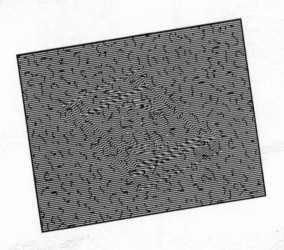

WHY DON'T MUMMIES TELL SECRETS?
BECAUSE THEY KEEP THINGS UNDER WRAPS!

INSERT THIS CHIP INTO MORPH. IT WILL TAKE YOU
WHERE YOU NEED TO GO.
A MEMBER OF YOUR FAMILY IS IN GREAT DANGER.
YOU NEED TO RESCUE THEM.

I left Stanley and the portrait of Henrietta on the landing and rushed to my room. As I plugged the chip into Morph, I could hardly believe my eyes when I saw the words that popped up on the computer screen...

Time Machine

"Grandpa!!!!!!" I screamed at the top of my lungs before bolting out of the room, and zooming past Stanley. I flew down the stairs and ran into the kitchen.

"Henry, calm down!" Grandpa said in alarm.

"I'm not Henry, I'm Will," I started, but there wasn't time for all that now. "You'll be able to speak to Henry yourself soon." I spoke so fast, even Plato looked confused.

"Sit down, boy," Grandpa said. "What do you mean?"

Grandpa listened as I told him about the program for Morph that had just turned up and how I was going to use it to go back in time to rescue Mum and Dad from their dinosaur-infested jungle.

"Slow down, Egburt," Grandpa held his hand in the air. "Time machine or no time machine, you're not going anywhere until the morning."

I opened my mouth to protest but Grandpa got in there first. "You need a good night's sleep before you start an Adventure, believe me."

There was no point arguing with Grandpa. He'd been on a bazillion Adventures before so he knew what he was talking about.

Without complaining, I headed back up the stairs to my bedroom. But when I got into bed, I couldn't get to sleep. I was so excited. Seconds seemed like minutes, minutes seemed like hours, and the hours felt like every French lesson I've ever sat through – never-ending.

My alarm buzzed to life at six o'clock the next morning and I ran downstairs to the kitchen to pack food for my Adventure.

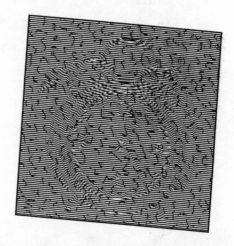

"I've made you a packed lunch," Grandpa said proudly. "Banana and ham sandwiches, pickled toffee and honey-coated liver. No grandson of mine is going back in time on an empty stomach."

"Er, thanks," I said as I took the bag from him.

Gobbling down a couple of slices of toast for breakfast, I then ran upstairs to get ready for my Adventure.

Mum and Dad were stuck in a prehistoric jungle full of dinosaurs, and going back to rescue them was going to be a dangerous mission. It was time to pack some survival supplies:

- Grandpa's spy journal
- Mosquito repellent (mozzies are everywhere in the jungle)
- Stun gun to fight off dinosaurs
- A small mirror (to check my hair wasn't too messy, so Mum wouldn't moan at me)

My Grandpa is soooo cool!

Only one more thing to take: my amulet. It was already around my neck, heavy and solid and a total mystery. It had been inside one of the letters and had saved my butt on the Dare space satellite when I was fighting the Partek. It had opened a door which had the same strange design.

I changed into my best, non-ripped jeans and favourite T-shirt. I hadn't seen Mum and Dad for months and I wanted to look my best.

Then I sat down to look at a section of Grandpa's spy journal. Reading about people who have been on Adventures before makes me feel braver.

What a stunner! he! he! →

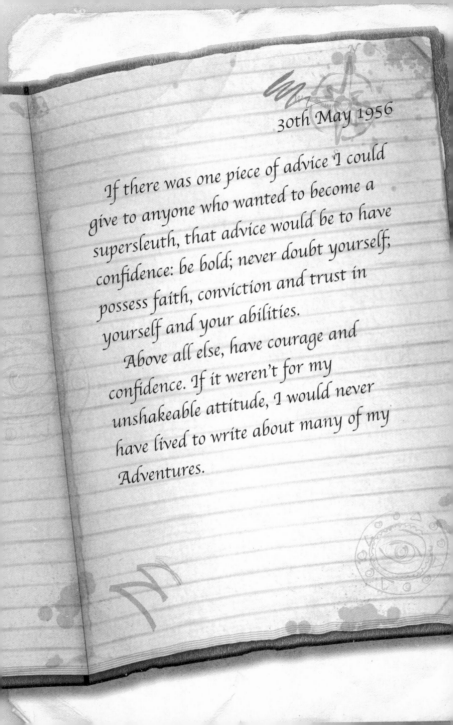

30th May 1956

If there was one piece of advice I could give to anyone who wanted to become a supersleuth, that advice would be to have confidence: be bold; never doubt yourself; possess faith, conviction and trust in yourself and your abilities.

Above all else, have courage and confidence. If it weren't for my unshakeable attitude, I would never have lived to write about many of my Adventures.

It was time to go. Grandpa and Plato followed me outside.

I plugged the time machine program into Morph and activated it.

Morph shook and spun before morphing into a brand-new time machine as Plato bounded forward.

"You can't come," I grinned. "A dangerous jungle is no place for a dog!"

"Let him go with you," said Grandpa. "Just bring him home in one piece."

And with that, the time machine door shut behind me or, rather, us.

Fingers trembling, I reached for the keyboard, just as the air around me changed; somehow every molecule began to glow, to fizz with energy like a freshly poured Cola. The fizzing grew and a million blinding white beams formed. Before

fizz fizz fizz

finally squeezing my eyes shut, I saw the beams twist together. One thing was for sure – this was time travel just like I remembered – and it would never, ever get boring! Maybe Morph already knew where Mum and Dad were. Was our destination already on the computer chip? I sure hoped so, as we seemed to fall further and further through the centre of the universe.

Eventually, the time machine stopped spinning and plonked itself down on the ground.

When I stopped feeling like I was going to throw up all over Morph, I took a deep breath and turned to Plato. "Ready to out-run some dinosaurs?"

He yapped at me and wagged his tail, as if he understood.

With my trusty stun gun in my hand, I psyched myself up about going into the jungle.

A billion thoughts ran through my mind. Would Mum and Dad be waiting outside? Would I have to go far to find them? Only one way to find out... I opened the time machine door.

As I stepped outside, I expected to tread on bracken and mud, but instead I was standing on golden sand! The air wasn't humid like a jungle, but dry like a desert.

It was really, really hot – hotter than sitting next to a bonfire. Sticky sweat was pouring off me and soaking through my clothes.

There were no sounds of pterodactyls overhead, or the thundering steps of a T-rex in the distance. All I could hear was the sound of the wind and Plato, panting beside me in the heat. There wasn't a prehistoric jungle in sight – only miles and miles and miles of sand. Morph had taken me to the wrong place!

There was movement in the sand and I looked down to see Plato digging at something. Beneath his paws there was the corner of a white envelope.

I bent down to pick it up. Plato must have thought I was playing some kind of game as he bit the other corner of the envelope and tried to wrestle it from me.

"No!" I shouted. But shouting only made him tug harder.

The envelope twisted as I pulled and pulled but Plato just wouldn't let go. Suddenly, I heard a massive ripping noise and I flew backwards, landing on my backside in the sand. Only half of the envelope was in my hand. The other half was being chewed up in Plato's mouth.

"PLATO!" I screamed as my instructions became a chewy, mushy mess.

Aaarrgghhh!

"I'm never taking you on an Adventure again!" I told him. But Plato just wagged his tail.

I tried my best to read the letter, even though half of it was covered in dog slobber.

WHAT DID KING TUT SAY WHEN HE HAD A NIGHTMARE?
I WANT MY MUMMY!

As you might have guessed, you're not in a prehistoric jungle. You're in a desert. The Sahara desert, to be precise. Morph has taken you where you needed to go. Not where you wanted to go.

A member of your family is in trouble.

The Solvit family will be plunged into peril unless

The rest of the letter was unreadable.

"Well, thanks a lot, Plato," I huffed. "Now I'm stuck in a desert with no clue where to go and nothing but a stun gun to help me. What am I meant to stun – the sand?"

Plato looked up at me with big black eyes and a wagging tail.

"Never mind," I said, sitting down next to him on the hot sand. "I guess we'll just have to wait here until I work something out."

The sun was beating down hard but there wasn't any shade in sight. I tried to think.

Suddenly, I spotted something moving in the distance. I squinted harder, narrowing my eyes. It was just a tiny speck... As the speck turned into a shape, I held my breath. It was getting closer and closer, and now I could see that the shape was a man. And he was heading straight for us.

In fact, the man turned out to be a boy. A boy who wasn't much older than me. He had short, curly blonde hair and was wearing trousers, a shirt and tie – weird clothes to be wearing in a desert.

He wasn't alone. There were three other people walking in single file behind him – that's why I hadn't been able to see them at first. It was as though the boy was leading them somewhere. The first man was short and fat and had a moustache like that of a walrus. The second man had thick glasses and carried a leather bag, and the third was tall and thin and wearing a red bow tie.

They walked up to me as I stood up, hiding the

stun gun behind my back – I didn't want them to think I was going to shoot them.

"Who are you?" the boy asked me. "And why are you dressed in such odd clothes?"

I thought that was a bit cheeky, bearing in mind what he was wearing.

"Who am I?" I started, feeling the need to defend myself. "Who are you?"

"I'm George Solvit, of course," the boy said proudly. "And I'm here on an official Adventure."

"Excuse me?" I asked, stunned. As far as I knew, I was the only Solvit Adventurer.

"I can see by the amulet you're wearing that you know exactly why we're here," George said, pointing to my neck.

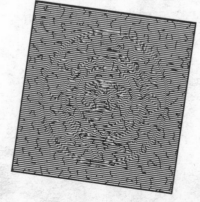

What? I had no idea what he was going on about. Then a thought struck me: my Adventure had taken me back in time to help out a family member. Maybe George was that family member!

"What year is it?" I asked.

The boy snorted at me as if I was mad. "Nineteen thirty-one, of course. Now, who exactly are you?"

Was I meant to tell him the truth? Maybe George wouldn't want me to help him.

"I'm Will," I said. I didn't tell him my surname – I didn't mind telling George who I was, but I didn't want the men he was with to know I was a time-travelling Adventurer from the 21st century. Who knows what they'd do if they found out. "And this is Plato," I said, pointing at my dog.

Plato yapped and wagged his tail.

"This is Mr Adam James, a labourer," said

George, introducing the short man with the moustache. "Dr Bill Wright, a doctor," he went on as the man wearing the thick glasses took a small bow. "And Mr Phillip Bottle, a journalist," George finished with the tall, thin man with the bow tie.

I shook everyone's hands as the introductions were made.

"We're in the Sahara to excavate the tomb of Queen Tiy," George started again. "It's a top-secret expedition. My companions have been sworn to secrecy. Mr James is here to dig, Dr Wright will make sure none of us gets sick and Mr Bottle is here to write about all of the wonderful discoveries we make in the tomb. My special skill is Egyptology – I'm here to translate the hieroglyphics on the tomb walls. Why are you here?"

I had to think on my feet, and fast. "Er...well,

I...I've been sent by the British government to help you," I said quickly, lying through my teeth. "My dog, Plato, has been specially trained to search for Egyptian artefacts."

George seemed happy with this and smiled. "Marvellous!" he exclaimed. "Well, let's not stand around in a scorching desert when there are cursed tombs to be uncovered."

"Whoa – rewind. Cursed?" I gasped. No one had said anything about strolling into a cursed Egyptian tomb.

"The British government hasn't informed you of the curse of Queen Tiy?"

George seemed surprised as I shook my head. "Well, I'll just have to fill you in as we walk," he said. "Mr James – lead the way!"

We followed the labourer further into the desert until my skin was burning. The more we walked, the hotter it became and I was desperate for a drink. Trudging along on sand was thirsty work. But I didn't have the chance to say anything because now George had started to talk again.

"Tiy was born during the reign of the great Egyptian Amarna Dynasty," he explained as we walked towards her tomb. "Her parents were the High Priest and Priestess of the cult of Anubis – the Egyptian jackal-headed god."

I nodded, as if I knew what he was going on about, and George seemed happy to go on...

"As a baby, Tiy was betrothed to the prince of Egypt," he continued. "When she grew up, Tiy married the prince. He became the Pharaoh and she was his queen. But, during the Pharaoh's reign, the whole kingdom was plunged into peril. Crops dried up and people starved. Plagues of insects swarmed around the Nile and spread

Gulp!

disease. Then the Pharaoh died in a horrible accident. Legend has it that when Queen Tiy died, a curse was put on her tomb. Her tomb was uncovered fifty years ago and every member of the excavation party dropped dead. A recovery party was sent inside to bring back the bodies but they also died. Every single person who's ever been into the tomb has died instantly."

"DIED?" I shouted out loud. This was suddenly getting serious.

"Yes, died," said George, looking puzzled by my reaction. "We've been sent to lift the curse and discover why it was put there in the first place."

Suddenly, the three men ahead of us stopped in their tracks. Mr Bottle was pointing to something in the distance. I tried to spot what he was pointing at, but all I could see was a large mound of sand. There wasn't anything else for miles –

not a blade of grass, not a tree, nothing – but
the doctor seemed to be getting more and more
excited. As we walked forward a few more steps,
the wind died down and now I could see what all
the fuss had been about. Golden grains of sand
swept away from the mound to reveal a door.

"There it is!" Mr James shouted. "It's the
entrance to Queen Tiy's tomb!"

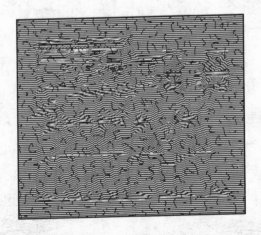

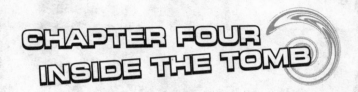

OK, so sometimes it's fun being an Adventurer but sometimes it isn't and, at that precise moment in time (1931 to be exact), it really wasn't... I was:

- standing in a scorching hot desert
- about to stroll into a cursed tomb
- hanging out with a boy who was nearly a hundred years older than me
- wishing I'd paid more attention in history lessons!

As I walked towards the tomb, I saw the door was covered in weird Egyptian symbols and there was the picture of a creature who had the body of a human but the head of a dog.

WOOF WOOF!

49

"Arggggggggh," I screamed, madly trying to dodge the snakes and make it out in one piece.

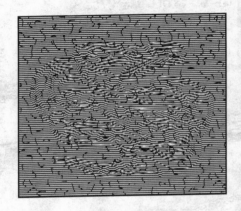

And it only got worse. We had to build a bridge to cross a chasm the size of a river, and George even had to translate an ancient poem about Osiris, the Egyptian god of the dead, before he could work out which way we needed to go.

Finally, we came to the door of the inner tomb. The darkness made me squint and my heart pounded with fear.

"When we walk in, we'll be dead men," Mr Bottle stuttered in a whisper.

I've never seen a grown-up look or sound

so scared.

"There's no such thing as a curse!" Dr Wright said.

And, before we could stop him, he walked straight into the tomb.

I held my breath, feeling my heart thud like a yeti's footsteps.

We waited for the sound of screaming.

We waited...and waited...and waited.

"This is ridiculous!" Mr James said suddenly. "We're standing around and he's in there taking all the gold for himself. I'm going in!"

George tried to hold him back, but it was too late. Mr James ran into the tomb and we were left in silence.

"Me too!" said Mr Bottle, who then also disappeared into the tomb.

"Why are they all so keen to go in there when

they're only going to drop dead?" I asked in bewilderment.

George looked at me with wild eyes. I could tell he was thinking something crazy.

"What if they're not going to drop dead?" he said. "What if there's no such thing as a cursed tomb? What if people only made it up to keep the gold safe?"

"George, I don't think we should..." but there was no point in arguing. He ran into the tomb before I had a chance to stop him.

I had no choice. I bolted after George, leaving Plato to follow me...

Beautiful is a funny kind of word to describe a tomb but it really was the only word I could come up with for the inside of Queen Tiy's last resting place. Gold statues lined the room, along with a multitude of chariots and there were enough gold tables and chairs to feed an army.

As I gazed around the room, I couldn't help but look in wonder at all the precious jewels, in every colour of the rainbow. Gold and jewels shimmered everywhere.

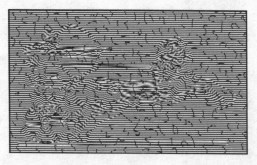

Pictures covered the walls, telling some kind of story about people starving, crops dying, and people fighting each other. There was an image of an Egyptian Queen looking down on all the pictures – it looked as though she was laughing, like she was causing all the horrible things. Whoever Queen Tiy was, she must have been a mega-mean lady.

The sight of the tomb was so incredible it took me a while to notice the dead bodies of Mr James, Dr Wright and Mr Bottle.

"George, I think they're..." I heard a thud behind me.

I ran over to where George was now crumpled in a heap on the floor. He wasn't moving. His eyes were shut and his body lay limp. I'd never seen a dead body before, let alone four of them. I felt a shiver run down my spine.

"George, George!" I screamed desperately. But George was stone-cold. I shook him and poured water over his face, but he still wouldn't move. Plato yapped and whined, putting his tail between

O.M.G.!!

his legs.

I knew how Plato felt – I was terrified too.

One thing I knew for certain – curses definitely existed and this curse was working to the max – it was killing off everything around me, which could mean only one thing. I was next!

I panicked – I didn't want to die. There was still so much I wanted to do: find Mum and Dad, see my pet dinosaur, Rex, again, climb Everest...

My sweaty feet slipped inside my trainers as I legged it towards the door. I needed to get out of there, and fast.

Running as quickly as I could down the corridors, I turned the corner to see the entrance. Daylight! But, just as I was within striking distance of it, the stone door slammed shut. I rattled and shook it but it wouldn't budge – I was stuck – stuck in the cursed tomb surrounded by dead bodies.

Putting my head in my hands, I let out a deep breath before looking up to see something carved in the back of the tomb door. It wasn't ancient Egyptian symbols like everything else in the tomb – it looked very like words written in English and in writing I'd recognize anywhere. It was the same lettering all my other letters were written in. I took a step closer to read the message.

WHY WERE ANCIENT EGYPTIAN CHILDREN CONFUSED?
BECAUSE THEIR DADDIES WERE MUMMIES!

YOU'RE SAFE FROM THE CURSE – FOR NOW.
TO FIND QUEEN TIY'S COFFIN, LOOK IN THE POT WITH THE MONKEY'S HEAD. TAKE WHATEVER YOU NEED.

THERE'S A FIGHT AHEAD.

LIFT THE LID OF QUEEN TIY'S COFFIN AND OPEN THE JAR
WITH THE JACKAL'S HEAD.

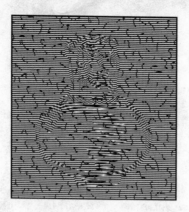

Plato whimpered loudly.

"It's OK," I told him, although I was feeling anything but OK. Still, I couldn't let Plato see that. "We'll be fine," I said. "All we've got to do is lift an ancient curse, bring people back from the dead and then go home to Grandpa."

It sounded simple, but I knew it wouldn't be. Turning around I saw a golden pot with a monkey's head. I took the lid off and looked inside to see a series of letters.

Using the alphabet that George had given me earlier, I translated the message. It simply read 'behind the statue'.

I looked desperately around the room until my eyes landed on a huge golden statue of some sort of man with a jackal's head. But before I looked behind the statue, I needed to prepare for a fight! The message on the tomb door had warned me of that. Looking around the room, my eyes landed on a golden spear, a golden axe and a golden bow and arrow. Those would just have to do.

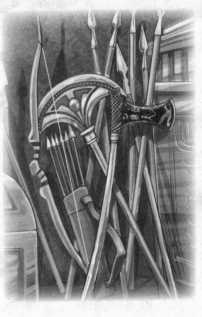

Loaded up with the weapons, I headed towards the statue. It was so heavy that I had to put everything down and use both hands to move it. My heart sank. There was no door behind the statue – just a wall covered with more Egyptian symbols. Using my list of Egyptian hieroglyphs, I translated them:

She sleeps behind me.

I'd read a comic book once where someone had built a wall around a radioactive bomb so that no one knew it was there. Only the wall wasn't made of bricks or stone, it was made of thin plaster and the hero kicked it in easily and stopped the world from being blown up. If kicking down a wall worked in comics, maybe I should give it a go?

Taking a run at it, I landed a flying kick on the wall – and I was right. It was made of carefully placed, weaker stones that collapsed easily into a massive heap. I landed on top, feeling slightly bruised but pleased with myself. The stones had fallen to reveal a tunnel!

George had dropped his flaming torch when he'd fallen to the ground so I picked it up and used it to look into the dark tunnel.

What I could see was seriously creepy. The walls were covered in paintings and there were coffins pressed against the tunnel. I tried to concentrate on what was ahead of me and not freak out about the sight of the dead bodies lying a few centimetres away.

The sound of coffin doors creaking open rang in my ears, making the hairs on my arms stick up like pokers. Then I heard the sound of croaking and moaning coming from the tunnel. It sounded like something had woken up from a long sleep and wasn't happy to be awake.

"Come on, Plato," I said, trying to sound brave as I picked up as many weapons as I could carry.

"Let's see what's going on in there."

Nervously, I stepped into the dark tunnel with Plato following on behind me, whimpering loudly. The ground was dusty and smelt rancid. My legs were shaking like jelly and I felt sick with fear.

The wailing got louder, and louder and louder…

I heard a shuffling in the darkness.

Then there was a shadow in the gloom…

It lurched towards me, its eyes glowing through the bandages like hot coals.

It was an Egyptian mummy. And it was headed straight for us!

"Plato, RUN!" I shouted at the top of my voice.

But it was too late. Before we could leg it, three more mummies had come to life around us.

Throwing the axe, I knocked the first mummy's head off, then made a swift retreat.

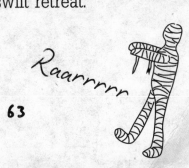

Raarrrrr

Will's fact file

Dear Adventurer,

For hundreds of years, mysteries of the ancient Egyptians have fascinated us. Why did they mummify people and worship strange gods? Where did their stories of gods and the afterlife come from? Who built the pyramids?

Well, if you don't mind a little bit of mud and dirt then maybe digging up the mysteries of ancient civilizations is your kind of Adventure!

Mummification Manual

As any ancient Egyptian knows, there's no crossing into the glorious afterlife unless your body is intact.

1. Make sure the body being mummified is 100% dead, then take it to a mortuary temple.

2. Find a priest wearing an Anubis mask to help with the mummification process.

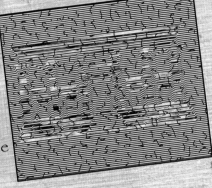

3. Wash the body in wine and Nile water.

4. Cut a hole in the side of the body and pull out the internal organs. This is very important – if you don't remove a person's insides, they'll rot.

5. Insert a hook through the nose and pull out the brains.

6. Cover the body with a special powder called natron. Leave it for 40 days to dry out.

7. Wash the body again with Nile water then stuff it with leaves sand and sawdust to make it look as life-like as possible.

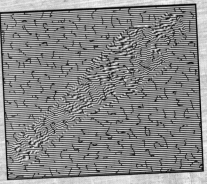

8. Wrap the body in linen strips. Hide precious stones between the strips to protect the body in the afterlife.

Burial for Beginners

For an authentic Egyptian burial, gather up your sacrifices and follow the instructions below.

1. Carefully place your mummified body into a wooden coffin.

2. Place the wooden coffin inside a solid gold coffin.

3. Put the gold coffin inside a large stone coffin.

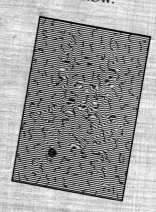

4. Place the stone coffin inside a tomb in the Valley of the Kings in Egypt.

5. Lead a large procession into the tomb. People should bring offerings such as food, furniture, gold statues or mummified pets.

6. Place the offerings in the tomb. These will help the dead person in the afterlife.

7. Decorate the tomb walls with paintings of things the person did in their life and things they'll be doing in the afterlife.

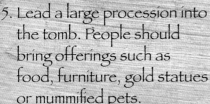

8. If the dead person is really important, bury them with models of their slaves. These will most likely come to life later on and help the dead person in the afterlife.

The Evening News

SUNDAY, NOVEMBER 5th 1922

TOMB OF BOY PHARAOH DISCOVERED!

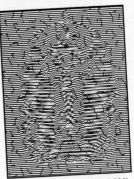

TUTANKHAMUN'S SOLID GOLD DEATH MASK

Yesterday, after years of hard digging, Howard Carter and his team of Egyptologists finally uncovered the lost tomb of Tutankhamun. Buried deep in the Valley of the Kings, the last resting place of the young king has amazed the archaeologists with its mind-blowing splendour.

For over 3,000 years, the gold statues, priceless jewels, weapons, games and chariots of Tutankhamun have remained undiscovered. But now a major excavation is taking place to recover the treasures from the tomb so the world can begin to unravel the secrets of the ancient Egyptians.

According to reports from the time, Tutankhamun was only 18 when he died after a blow to the head. He had been crowned Pharaoh when he was only nine years old.

Story continues on next page.

Did you know? Queen Tiy was Tutankhamun's grandmother!

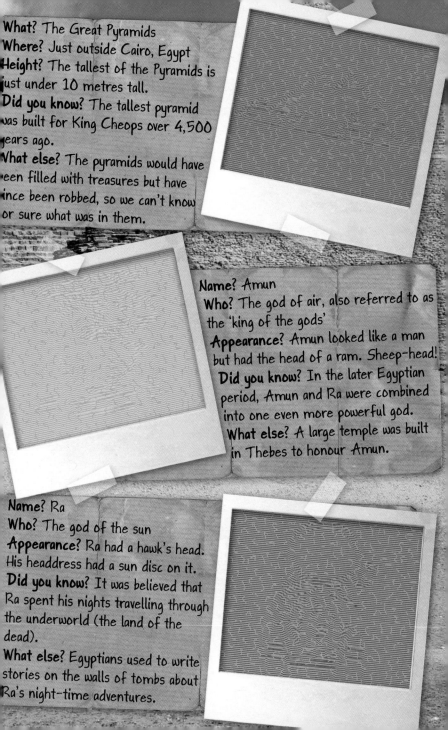

What? The Great Pyramids
Where? Just outside Cairo, Egypt
Height? The tallest of the Pyramids is just under 10 metres tall.
Did you know? The tallest pyramid was built for King Cheops over 4,500 years ago.
What else? The pyramids would have been filled with treasures but have since been robbed, so we can't know for sure what was in them.

Name? Amun
Who? The god of air, also referred to as the 'king of the gods'
Appearance? Amun looked like a man but had the head of a ram. Sheep-head!
Did you know? In the later Egyptian period, Amun and Ra were combined into one even more powerful god.
What else? A large temple was built in Thebes to honour Amun.

Name? Ra
Who? The god of the sun
Appearance? Ra had a hawk's head. His headdress had a sun disc on it.
Did you know? It was believed that Ra spent his nights travelling through the underworld (the land of the dead).
What else? Egyptians used to write stories on the walls of tombs about Ra's night-time adventures.

Name? Osiris
Who? The ancient Egyptian god of the dead and ruler of the underworld
Appearance? Osiris had a big beard and a cone head.
Did you know? Osiris's skin was green because he was dead and his flesh was rotting.
What else? Egyptians believed that after people died, they would travel to the underworld to live with Osiris

Name? Isis
Who? The goddess of protection, using powerful magic spells to help people
Appearance? Isis was female and had a headdress in the shape of a throne.
Did you know? The high priestesses of Isis were doctors and midwives. It is said they could interpret dreams and control the weather.
What else? Isis protected the dead body of a Pharaoh.

Name? Anubis
Who? The god of mummies
Appearance? Anubis had the head of a jackal.
Did you know? Jackals used to roam around ancient Egyptian cemeteries. Egyptians believed that jackals watch over the dead.
What else? The Egyptians also believed Anubis would watch over people as they were mummified

Name? Horus

Who? Ancient Egyptian god of the sky and protector of Egypt

Appearance? Horus looked like a man with the head of a falcon. Egyptians believed one of his eyes was the sun and the other was the moon.

Did you know? A temple was dedicated to Horus in Egypt at Edfu.

What else? Horus was believed to be the son of Isis and Osiris.

Name? Thoth

Who? God of writing, knowledge and wisdom

Appearance? Thoth was usually portrayed as a man with the head of an ibis bird. But sometimes he was drawn as a baboon — identity crisis!

Did you know? Egyptians believed Thoth invented hieroglyphics.

What else? Millions of ibis birds were sacrificed for Thoth.

Name? Sobek

Who? God of the Nile and protector of the Pharaoh

Appearance? Sobek had the head of a crocodile. Croc-face!

Did you know? Egyptians thought if they worshipped a crocodile-headed god, they were less likely to get eaten by the crocodiles in the Nile!

What else? Egyptians kept crocodiles in pools at temples to honour Sobek.

The Solvit Hall of Egyptology

Philip Solvit

Philip was an adviser to Alexander the Great. Together, the two men conquered most of the known world over two thousand years ago. Philip lived in a small house by the Nile and kept a pet crocodile called Craig.

George Solvit *George*

George Solvit was one of the greatest Egyptologists who ever lived. By the age of five he was fluent in hieroglyphics and made his first discovery of a tomb when he was ten.

Monty Solvit

Towards the end of the Second World War, Monty Solvit was sent to spy on criminals in Egypt. Whilst he was there he stayed with an elderly man who claimed to have been alive for over 3,000 years. The old man told Monty many tales of ancient Egypt and Monty wrote about them in his journal.

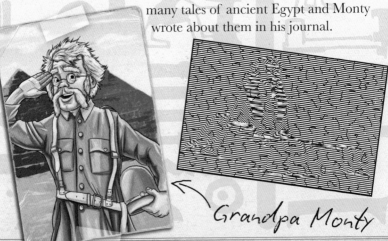

Grandpa Monty

"Nice work," I said to Plato. He was only small but he'd fought as bravely as any Adventurer.

Plato gave a small bark in appreciation.

Walking into the darkness, we headed towards the inner burial chamber. I lifted the torch flame above my head. There were more horrible paintings on the walls and a huge stone coffin was in the middle of the room.

I was just about to start pushing the stone lid aside when I heard a soft thud at my feet.

A knot caught in my throat and I felt like someone was squeezing my heart – I couldn't breathe.

Next to my feet, Plato's limp little body was lying on the floor. The curse had got to him too!

"Plato... Plato, wake up!"

I wanted to scream and cry and shout at the top of my voice. I wanted to go back to the other room and smash every statue, pot and picture to pieces. I wanted the mummies to come back and fight me so I could bash their brains out again. Plato was dead and it was all my fault – I hadn't protected him from the curse of Queen Tiy. What would Grandpa say? He had trusted me with him.

What could I do? There wasn't anything that could bring Plato back to life. Unless... Just at that moment I had the tiniest inkling of an idea. What if I could go back in time and stop the curse from ever being put on the tomb? It sounded crazy but it might just work. After all, Morph's time machine was working. Not only could I help Plato, I could save everyone: George, Mr James, Dr Wright and Mr Bottle. I was their only hope.

Trying not to get upset, I swallowed hard and blinked away the tears. The coffin lid was heavy, but I had so much anger flowing through my veins I didn't care how hard I had to try to get it open. The skin on my fingers ripped and bled as I pushed the stone lid aside.

Inside the stone coffin was another coffin, only this one was made of gold and covered in jewels. I didn't waste any time getting that open too.

And there she was.

Queen Tiy – the evil witch who had killed George and Plato and had cursed everyone who had ever stepped into her tomb. Her body was wrapped in bits of cloth that had so many hundreds of jewels sewn into it you could tell she must have been important.

But there was something else tucked into her bandages besides jewels – an envelope with my name on it.

I picked it up and ripped it open.

How does King Tut's secretary answer his calls?
"He can't talk right now, he's all wrapped up."

Don't let Plato's sacrifice be in vain. Avenge him. Avenge George and every other person who has stepped into this evil tomb. Next to Queen Tiy are four jars. Open the jar with the jackal's head.

Do as the letter inside tells you. It's the only way.

I fumbled around in the coffin to find the jars that the letter was talking about and sure enough, there was the one with the jackal's head. Carefully, I lifted up the lid and peered inside. It looked as though there was an ancient scroll inside, written in gold leaf. I pulled it out to take a look but I couldn't understand the Egyptian symbols. I took out the list of hieroglyphs George had given me and translated them... The words that were written sent a shiver down my spine...

Come back and save me.
You'll find me at sunset.

There was something else in the jar too – an amulet, pretty similar to the one I was wearing,

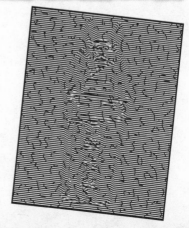

69

only this one was heavier than mine and covered in jewels.

As the amulet glinted and glistened in my hand, Morph seemed to buzz to life in my bag. I pulled it out and pressed my thumb against the activation pad. Morph shook and spun around, making a loud whirring sound as it sprung up into a time machine.

Taking a deep breath, I climbed inside and closed the door behind me, hoping it would take me where I needed to go...

I was so pleased to be stepping into that machine. I needed to get away from the scene that lay behind me and only by going back in time might I have a chance to make things right...

The skin on my face rippled like raspberry ripple ice cream as I swished and swirled through the air, somersaulting as we zoomed back in time. But finally we seemed to be slowing and then, before I knew it, Morph had slowed to a standstill. With a sudden jolt, I flew to the floor.

Picking myself up, I just had a moment to catch my breath before I opened the time machine door. Hesitantly, I gazed outside – I was standing on the banks of a wide river – you didn't have to be Einstein to guess that the river was the Nile.

I had done a project on rivers at my old school and had learnt a lot of stuff about it, such as…

SNAP! SNAP!

- The Nile is the longest river in the world.
- The crocodiles in the Nile are the largest in Africa.
- Nile boats were the main form of transportation for the ancient Egyptians.

There were some sailboats floating along the water, manned by people with shoulder-length black hair and wearing white cloths around their waists. They looked just like the people in the pictures on the walls of Queen Tiy's tomb, so at least I had come back to the right era.

On the other side of the river was the most amazing building imaginable with pillars that towered into the sky. It looked like it could be a temple and was more eye-poppingly awesome than any skyscraper I'd ever seen. In front of the building was a row of weird-looking statues that each had the body of a lion but the head of a man wearing an Egyptian headdress – similar to the pictures I'd seen back in the tomb. They were bigger than Grandpa Monty's house, if that were possible. Around the temple, dozens of people were walking about – all wearing white cloths around their waists and big gold chains around their necks.

I gulped. It didn't feel like I'd gone back in time – I felt like Morph had taken me to another world. But I wasn't there to sightsee – I had a job to do!

The sun was low in the sky, about to disappear behind the temple, when a marching sound came from behind me.

As I turned around to see what was going on, something weird happened. The amulet around my neck started to glow like a fire. It turned a bright red colour and felt really warm against my skin. I'd never seen it do anything like that before.

Sounds of chanting filled my ears. There were about twenty people walking in my direction, all marching in some kind of procession.

At the front was a man wafting incense around. Behind him were other men and women carrying plates of food and golden weapons. In the middle of the party there were six strong-looking men carrying a platform that had a woman and a girl aboard. They were sitting on golden thrones and had people fanning them with green leaves.

"Halt!" the woman on the platform finally commanded. "Lower me, servants!"

What kind of woman has servants carrying her around all day? A pretty important one, that's for sure.

And then I had a sudden thought. I'd just understood what the woman had said and yet surely she'd be speaking ancient Egyptian and not

English! So why could I understand her?

Carefully the men laid the platform down on the ground and the woman stepped off. She was wearing golden sandals and had a golden snake bracelet on her arm. Even her clothes looked like they'd been spun from pure gold! The lady's hair was braided with beads at the end so that they made a sound like a pair of maracas as she walked towards me.

"What are you?" she asked.

At that moment I realized a serious glitch in my plan. It would have been a sensible idea to think carefully about travelling back to ancient Egypt in my present clothes. I should have made myself invisible, or at least tried to hide myself before I'd had a chance to change. Certainly I should have made more of an effort not to walk straight up to the first Egyptian I came across. But my mind had been so caught up with Plato and George dying that the sensible part of it had turned to banana mush.

"Er...er...I'm Will," I said to her.

The words that came out of my mouth weren't English. They sounded old and ancient and were completely foreign to me – I was speaking a long-lost language. Ancient Egyptian was clearly coming out of my mouth, but I had no idea how! The amulet around my neck burned into my skin like fire, like it had come to life. And then a light bulb lit up in my brain – the amulet was obviously helping me to speak Egyptian!

The Egyptian woman looked at me like I smelled of farts.

"Are you human?" she said. "Your hair... your clothes...the things you carry...you look like nothing I've ever seen before."

Ouucchhh!

"I'm human," I nodded. "But I'm not from around here."

"So you're a gift from Anubis?" she asked.

I raised an eyebrow. "Anu who?"

"Anubis – our god," she explained.

The idea of being a gift from a god didn't sound too bad to me so I just agreed and nodded. She must have liked my answer because her face split into a massive smile.

"Pleased to meet you. I am the High Priestess of the Temple of Anubis," she said gently.

Now, if I remembered rightly, George told me that Tiy's mother was a priestess of Anubis. So if that lady was the High Priestess of Anubis then she must be Tiy's mother. And if she was Tiy's mum, then I'd bet a year's supply of bubble gum that the girl she was travelling with was Tiy! Bingo!

"Is that Queen Tiy?" I asked the lady, pointing to the girl sitting on the golden throne.

The lady laughed at me and said, "She will be soon. My precious darling's wedding to the Pharaoh is in eight days."

Wow! Egyptians obviously like to marry young – Tiy didn't look much older than me!

"You must be hungry," the Priestess said, changing the subject.

I nodded. I was starving and, although I really wanted to help George, Plato and the others, I wasn't going to be much use to anyone on an empty stomach.

The lady led me back to the platform that Tiy was sitting on, and I stepped onto it and sat down next to the young girl. The Priestess sat on her throne and her servants lifted us into the air before carrying us towards the Nile.

There was a boat waiting for us at the water's edge and, as we climbed down, I seized the opportunity to speak to Tiy. If I wanted to find out what the curse was all about I had to make friends with her and making her laugh with a joke might just do the trick.

It wouldn't be easy though – her face was screwed up like a shrivelled grape and her arms were folded across her chest like she was in a really bad mood.

"Er... What's the difference between bogeys and cabbage?" I asked, desperate to get her attention. But now Tiy was looking at me in disgust, so all I could do was give the punchline. "Kids don't eat cabbage!" I forced a laugh.

"Silence, donkey boy!" Tiy held up her hand. "Why would you laugh when you've been sent here by Anubis?"

Donkey boy →

"Well, who wouldn't want to be a gift from a god?" I started.

A slow smile stretched across Tiy's face.

"Anubis is the god of mummies," Tiy explained. "If he has sent you to us it's because you will be sacrificed. My parents are going to kill you!"

uh-oh!

"Kill me!" I gasped. "Why on earth would they want to do that? I mean, I'm no trouble. I...I'm just a boy. There must be better people to sacrifice?"

But it was too late to protest as our boat pulled up at the riverbank and a loud gong sounded. We climbed out of the boat. In front of us, an enormous pair of golden gates led into a temple. On either side stood bald-headed guards who had what looked like blood painted on their faces. They were holding sharp axes and spears.

Tiy and her mother led me through the gates. Inside the temple, hundreds of flaming torches lit the walls, but it was still dingy and dark. Everywhere I looked there were statues – statues

82

made of gold, statues made of stone, statues covered with jewels. And each of them had the same thing in common – they all had a man's body but a jackal's head – presumably Anubis.

Suddenly, the sound of trumpets filled the air and a group of servants carrying a grand throne walked out of the darkness at the back of the temple. There was a man with a bald head sitting aboard. He was wearing robes made out of exotic animal skin.

"Daddy!" Tiy shouted as she ran towards him. "Look what we've found," she said, pointing at me. "He's been sent here by Anubis."

"Er...actually," I said slowly, as I walked towards Tiy's father, the High Priest of Anubis, "there must have been some mistake. You see, I haven't been sent here by Anubis. I'm just a normal boy. No point killing me."

"You don't look very normal," the Priest said, eyeballing me from head to toe.

"I'll inform the others that we have a special guest this evening," Tiy's mother exclaimed, clapping her hands. "We'll have such a feast. Crocodile liver, hawk tongue and Nile fish eyes – only the best foods for our special sacrifice. A final meal fit for Anubis himself."

"Actually, I'm not too keen on crocodile liver..."

"Such spirit in the child!" said the Priest. "Tiy, take him to rest until the sun sets. We'll call you both when we are ready to feast."

So Tiy led me out of the main temple hall, down some corridors and into a small room.

"Stay here," Tiy said to me. "I'll be back for you soon."

"Wait!" I pleaded in a whisper. Tiy stopped and turned to look at me. "You have to help me. Getting sacrificed wasn't exactly what I had planned for today. If you help me then I'll help you in any way I can."

"You cannot help me, insect boy," Tiy laughed through gritted teeth. "I'm cursed, my whole life is cursed. And I'm going to curse everyone around me in return."

And she pulled out an amulet from underneath her clothes – the same amulet I'd seen in her tomb.

I pulled out mine from under my T-shirt. It was exactly the same as hers, only it wasn't covered in jewels.

"You have one too?" Tiy said, clearly surprised. "Who gave it to you?" she asked.

"Er… I kind of…inherited it," I told her.

"The old Pharaoh gave me mine," she said, her eyes filling up with tears and her voice trembling as she spoke. "He gave it to me when I became betrothed to his son. I was four years old at the time."

"You got engaged when you were four?" I gasped in shock.

"Yes," she explained. "Terrible, isn't it? My amulet has ancient magic flowing through it – I can use it for good or I can use it to curse. But curse it shall be. Why should I do anyone any good when no one cares about me?"

"I'm sure that's not true," I said. "I'm sure your parents care about you."

She laughed at me. "What would you know, turtle-breath? All they care about is that I marry some spotty idiot who smells like a toilet ditch!"

I couldn't help but laugh. Tiy was clearly insane but she was quite funny. Toilet ditch – good one!

Tiy's eyes flashed angrily as she spoke. "I hate

Tiy is sooo rude!

everyone: the King, my parents and our servants. If I can't be happy then no one will. I'm going to curse the Nile so it dries up and the plants stop growing. The people of Egypt will all die from plague and famine. I curse the Pharaoh who wants to marry me, the servants that look after me and every child I ever have.

"I'll even curse the tomb I'm buried in. No one will ever, ever be able to come near me without dropping dead!"

"Now hang on, wait a minute," I stepped in, holding up my hand. "That's kind of how I ended up here," I said. "I need you to lift that curse. People are going to die because of you...a lot of them."

Tiy's eyes narrowed. "Exactly, that's the point," she said.

I had to stop her. I had to convince her that

cursing everything wasn't the thing to do. "Look, don't you think you're over-reacting slightly? I mean, I'd be angry if someone tried to make me marry anyone – especially if it was someone who smelt like a toilet. But cursing everyone isn't going to help."

"Well, what do you suggest I do, goat boy?" Tiy fumed.

"Run away! Marry someone else! I don't know. Try talking to your parents; tell them you're too young?"

"Run away?" she said hopefully.

A plan was taking shape in my head as I spoke. "We could run away together?"

Tiy thought about it for a minute. "OK," she said finally. "You wait here. I'll go and get provisions: food, blankets and water."

She turned around and headed for the door.

"Bring lots of food," I shouted after her. "But no crocodile liver!"

At that moment, I was feeling like a weight had been taken off my shoulders. Not only had I managed to convince Tiy to run away with me (which meant I wasn't going to get killed and she didn't have to go around cursing people), but it would also mean that Plato and the others would be saved in the future. Could it really be as simple as this? As I sat, thinking about it all, my amulet pulsated against my neck. It could open locks and help me understand ancient languages – what else might it be able to do? Might it be able to bring back Mum and Dad?

Thoughts of magical amulets zoomed through my head as I sat there and waited for Tiy to come back. I waited and waited and waited. I paced up and down the room in panic. As I tried to calm myself, I sat down on the bed of straw and put my head in my hands.

But then something white caught my eye, poking out of the straw.

It was impossible! How could someone have left a letter for me in ancient Egypt? They didn't even have proper paper in those days!

But how the letter got there wasn't important – it was what the letter said that mattered. I tore open the envelope.

WHAT IS A MUMMY'S FAVOURITE TYPE OF MUSIC?

WRAP!

TIY HAS RUN AWAY WITHOUT YOU. DON'T WAIT FOR HER.
BUT DON'T WORRY, YOU'LL SEE HER AGAIN.
REMEMBER: MUMMIES CAN'T STAND THE SIGHT OF
THEMSELVES.

Tiy had run away without me! I'd hardly had time to translate the hieroglyphs in the letter before I heard footsteps tearing down the corridor towards me. Quickly, I shoved the letter into my pocket.

"Tiy!" I shouted hopefully.

But it wasn't Tiy at all. It was her mother and father, and they looked seriously worried.

"We found this in Tiy's room!" the High Priest shouted at me. His face had turned as red as a tomato as he held up a piece of parchment covered in hieroglyphs.

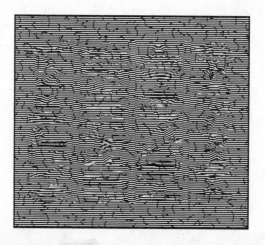

"What is it?" I asked him.

"It's a letter," he told me. "A letter that Tiy wrote to us, explaining how you had suggested she run away so she didn't have to get married."

Uh-oh. I tried to make a quick exit from the room but the Priest grabbed my T-shirt and hauled me back.

"You're not going anywhere!" he bellowed, flecks of his spit hitting my face as he shouted. His breath reeked like hippo farts.

The High Priestess studied me with worried eyes and then gasped as she said, "Everything is going wrong because Anubis is angry!"

"Why?" the Priest quizzed his wife.

"We should have sacrificed this boy as soon as we could and not put it off until tomorrow."

"You're right!" the Priest agreed.

I had to think on my feet if I was going to have

any chance of saving myself.

"No, she's not!" I said quickly. "Anubis is probably mad because you're going to sacrifice me full stop – let me go and find Tiy and..."

The Priest ignored me. "Take him into the heart of the temple and prepare to wake the mummies of Anubis!" he said to his wife as they dragged me out of the room and along the corridor.

"Tonight we will bring Tiy back to us. Tonight we will make Anubis happy. Tonight we will sacrifice this boy and let the undead suck the life from his veins!"

It wasn't looking good for me... Not good at all.

stinky bum!

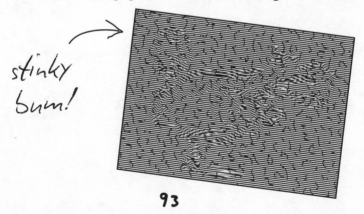

CHAPTER EIGHT
THE MUMMIES ATTACK

As the High Priest and Priestess of Anubis tied my hands behind my back, I felt a shiver run down my spine. I looked across the room and saw that my backpack was gone. Morph was in my bag! Without it I had no way to escape – I was mummy meat, for sure.

The only things I had in my pocket were bubble gum, the letter I'd found, some pennies and a mirror. What could I do? How could I convince them to save me?

Arguing with the High Priest and Priestess was no good. Before I could utter another word, they had gagged me and were dragging me outside into a colossal courtyard. The sun had completely set now, and in the middle of the square was what looked like a massive swimming pool – only people weren't swimming in it, there were hundreds of crocodiles thrashing around.

The High Priest led me onto a platform. I struggled and tried to escape but four bulky Egyptians came and held me still. Then the beating of a large drum sounded and a chorus of chanting started – the ceremony had begun.

People started to walk towards us from every direction, carrying torches to light their way. Snakes were pulled out of baskets as their masters began to charm them with pipes. The High Priest and Priestess put on jackal-headed masks.

"We call to great Anubis to accept this sacrifice," said the High Priest.

"Anubis, send your soldiers to us," said the High Priestess.

Arrrrrrgh!

And with that, the air was filled with the sound of groaning, just like the noises I'd heard before in Tiy's tomb, which could mean only one thing. Mummies!

"Arrrrrrrrgh," I let out a scream as they started to creep out of the shadows.

The ground cracked and mummies started to rise from beneath the ground. Some of them came out of the lake. Some of them came out of the temple. They were everywhere!

Then someone pushed me down and, before I knew it, I was lying on a stone slab, rock-hard beneath my back. It sent shudders down my spine and I thought I was going to be sick. What were they going to do? Turning my head, I watched in horror as the mummies closed in on me. Their rotten arms reached out and their eyes hung out of their sockets. Their mouths opened wide as they let out their hair-raising wails.

That was it – I had no way to escape. My life as an Adventurer was going to be over.

"Anubis, accept our humble sacrifice…" the Priestess had started saying. She was swaying as she spoke, like she was in some kind of trance. "Eat his heart and drink his soul…"

The mummies were so close I could smell their stinking breath. "Let his life open the gateway to the glorious dead…"

I was out of ideas and was staring death in the face – literally!

"Rip his beating heart from his chest and let its beat be the rhythm of your drum of death!" the Priestess wailed.

The zombie groaning was so loud that every part of my body was electrified with fear.

I like it
IN my chest,
thank you!

97

Tiy threw me a spear and we started fighting the mummies. It wasn't working — we were outnumbered!

We're mummy food!

Then I remembered the last line of my letter...

Grabbing the mirror from my pocket, I held it up to the nearest mummy. His eyes burst in his head and his body caught fire.

"Grab anything shiny and hold it up to the mummies!" I shouted to Tiy desperately.

Tiy grabbed a shard of glass and held it up to the nearest mummy. It worked! One by one they shrieked and burst into flames.

Finally, when they were all dead, I turned to Tiy. "Where were you?" I cried. "You just ran off and left me!"

"I was running away," she said sheepishly. "Then I thought about everything you said, and you were right. Cursing people isn't a nice thing to do. I should just be honest with my parents. And then I realized that Anubis didn't send you here to be sacrificed. He sent you here to help lift my curse – he sent you here to make me happy."

I was one hundred per cent sure it was Morph that had brought me back in time, not the god of mummies, but if that made me friends with Tiy and got me out of being killed then that was fine.

The High Priest and Priestess joined us.

"What's going on?" asked the High Priest, lifting off his mask. "Why did you run away, Tiy?"

"I'm so unhappy…" Tiy wailed as she told her father all about not wanting to marry the Pharaoh, and how it would ruin her life. "He smells worse than a toilet!" she finished, sobbing. "I put the curse on the mummies – I wanted them to kill you so I wouldn't have to marry him. But I changed my mind at the last minute – I couldn't watch you die – and they nearly killed me too!"

She told her parents about the amulet that the old Pharaoh had given her, and how she had planned to use it to curse everyone around her – including them.

"We had no idea you felt this way, darling," her mother said tearfully.

"But Tiy," her father said gently, "if you don't marry the Pharaoh, you'll bring shame upon our family and the cult of Anubis will be disgraced."

"Will you perhaps consider marrying him in a few years?" her mother joined in, trying to reason.

Tiy wrinkled her nose in thought. "Perhaps," she said. "But I'm not promising anything."

"At least promise you won't run away again?" her mother said.

"Only if you promise you won't kill my friend," Tiy said, pointing straight at me.

"Very well," her parents agreed.

"Phew!" I sighed, about to leave.

"Not so fast..." the High Priest said to me. "I will grant you freedom on one condition."

"Anything," I agreed quickly.

"You must answer the riddle of the Sphinx," he said grandly.

CHAPTER NINE
THE RIDDLE OF THE SPHINX

"The riddle of the Sphinx?" I gulped. How was I going to manage that? I walked out of the temple towards the banks of the Nile with Tiy and the High Priest and Priestess of Anubis.

The High Priest stopped beside a huge man-lion statue. He beckoned for me to go and stand next to him.

"Will you give me back my bag and let me go if I crack this riddle?" I asked timidly.

"I will set you free, yes," said the High Priest.

I breathed a sigh of relief. Still, how was I going to crack the riddle?

Tiy held my bag in her hands and swung it about, "I've never seen such an ugly bag before!"

She's never seen my teacher!!

she said. "No gold, no jewels – you must be so poor. I knew as soon as I met you that you were nothing but a little insect..."

"Excuse me," I said, knowing she was only teasing me, and so I teased her back. "If it wasn't for me you'd be served up on a plate as zombie food right now. And who are you calling 'insect', dung beetle!"

"Dung beetles are sacred animals to us," she smiled.

"Enough!" the High Priestess shouted, holding up her hand.

The High Priest turned to face the Sphinx and said, "It is time..."

The stone statue of the Sphinx suddenly moved to reveal eyes of gold. It opened its mouth to speak. "Who is the warrior attempting to solve the riddle of the Sphinx?" it asked.

"I am," I answered, straightening up to look as tall as possible.

"Answer it correctly," said the Sphinx, "and you will pass. Answer it incorrectly and you will die."

A shiver ran down my spine and beads of perspiration broke out on my forehead as the Sphinx continued.

"What has one voice, and goes from four legs, to two legs, to three legs?"

As far as riddles go, the riddle of the Sphinx was mega-tough. The sun started to rise over the horizon as I stood there and thought about it – no way did I want to get it wrong. My heart was thumping as I tried to figure out the answer.

What walks on two legs? As soon as I got that part of the riddle then the rest of it made sense too. I knew it – I knew the answer!

"A human!" I answered confidently. "Humans use four limbs when they crawl as a baby, two legs when they walk as an adult and three legs when they're old and need a walking stick."

"Correct," the Sphinx declared. "You may live."

I couldn't believe it! I had cracked the riddle. I literally jumped for joy. But I didn't get much of a chance to celebrate. The High Priest had summoned one of his servants from the bank of the river. The servant led Tiy and me down to the water where we stepped into a small boat and began to cross the river.

I spent the journey back across the river explaining who I was to Tiy.

"You're a time traveller!" Tiy said in disbelief.

"Yup," I replied.

The boat we were sailing on was getting closer to the far bank of the Nile so I didn't really have time to go into great detail. Besides, I was desperate to get back to Plato and the others.

"Do you have to go back now?" Tiy asked me. "Maybe you could stay and we could be friends. Maybe I could even marry you instead of the Pharaoh?"

"Nah, you're alright, thanks," I laughed awkwardly. "You wouldn't want to do that."

"No, perhaps you're right," Tiy smiled. "Although my family would give you the protection of Anubis and 10,000 camels!"

NO WAY!!!

"Er, no use for camels back home," I replied quickly, "but thanks anyway."

The Egyptian servants moored the boat on the riverside and Tiy and I hopped out – I couldn't

He's got the hump!

107

wait to get home. As we walked through the long grass on the riverbank and into the desert, I thought about everything that had happened.

"Around here will be fine," I said, pointing to the desert floor.

All I needed was a flat bit of ground to activate Morph, and where we were standing would do the trick.

Tiy watched in silence as I pulled Morph out of my bag. She gave a small scream as I activated it and then she jumped backwards as Morph sprung up into a huge time machine.

"Wow!" she exclaimed as Morph whizzed and whirled into life. Her eyes looked like they were about to explode.

"Better than a magic amulet?" I grinned at Tiy. She smiled back.

I was walking towards the time machine door,

about to say goodbye to Tiy, when she tugged on my arm and pulled me around to face her.

"Take me with you?" she said, her eyes welling up with tears.

"I don't think I can," I said. "It doesn't really work like that."

I didn't exactly know what the rules were about taking people out of their natural times – but if what happened with Rex was anything to go by then it probably wasn't a good idea. Tiy seemed to understand that, and stepped back a little.

"Will you promise to always remember me?" she asked. "Tell others about me. I don't want to be forgotten after I die."

"Of course I will," I replied. "Look, why don't we do a deal? How about I promise to remember you if you promise not to put any more curses on people?"

Tiy didn't say anything. Instead, she took the magic amulet from around her neck and placed it into my hands. "No more curses," she said. "And actually, I would like to give you two more things."

"OK," I said hesitantly.

"First, there's this," she said, placing half a gold coin in my hand.

"Where's the other half?" I asked.

"Don't be greedy," she laughed. "The coin will bring you luck. Keep it with you, always."

"What was the other thing – you said you wanted to give me two things?"

Her face turned bright red and she took a step towards me. She closed her eyes and pouted her lips, as if she wanted to kiss me.

I didn't know what to say – no one had wanted to kiss me before. I felt embarrassed.

Yuck!

Gross!

Phew!!

"Bye!" I said quickly, stumbling back towards Morph and shutting the door firmly behind me.

There wasn't a moment to spare. Morph had fired up and was lifting into the air. Before I knew it, I was whizzing through time again and clutching my stomach as my guts churned.

We landed with a bump and I opened the time machine door – I was back in Tiy's tomb, but it looked completely different this time. For one thing, the pictures on the wall had changed. People looked happy – there was no war, no famine. Tiy had clearly led a long and happy life.

There was a picture of Tiy as a grown woman, marrying the Pharaoh. They looked happy. I walked up to Tiy's coffin and looked at her mummy.

Carefully, I placed the amulet that she had given me onto the mummy's chest and closed the lid. The tunnel where I'd fought the zombie mummies was empty as I walked back through it.

Voices were coming from outside…they were arguing about who should go into the tomb first.

"Will, where have you been?" It was George. "I looked around and you'd just disappeared," he went on. "How can we get to work on lifting this curse if you just go off like that?" But he didn't wait for a reply – he stomped off ahead of me.

I smiled as Plato bounded up to me, his tail wagging happily.

"I think you might find it's already lifted," I said.

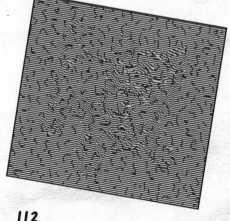

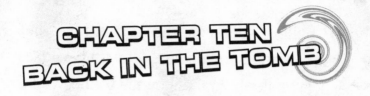

CHAPTER TEN
BACK IN THE TOMB

I was so relieved to see everyone alive again,
I told them everything, well, nearly everything.
I kept the bit about Tiy wanting to kiss me to
myself. That was too cringeworthy to share!

"So I jumped into the time machine, closed the
door and came back here," I finished.

Everyone was silent for a moment, then the
labourer, Mr James, spoke.

"I don't believe you!" he snorted.

"Well, I know an Adventurer when I see
one," George winked at me. "A time-travelling
Adventurer. Who would have thought there was
such a special skill?"

"A time-travelling Adventurer? Special skill?

I don't believe such nonsense," said Mr James.

Then George spoke again. "It's time to excavate Queen Tiy's tomb!" he announced. And with that, George and the others headed into the tomb.

I made the most of the opportunity to have a moment alone with Plato. I bent down and ruffled his shaggy white fur. Plato eagerly licked my hand and let out a happy little growl.

"Now you've got to promise not to go getting yourself killed again," I told him. "Then I'll take you Adventuring!"

Plato yapped and wagged his tail as I walked into Queen Tiy's tomb, thankful not to see a room full of dead bodies. Instead, George, Mr James and the others were all walking about, making notes and taking pictures of everything they saw.

"What's going to happen to all this stuff?" I asked them.

"Everything will be catalogued and taken to a museum," George told me as he picked up a small golden statue and examined it closely.

His face suddenly went pale. "You...you don't think she'd mind us taking things from her tomb, do you?"

A smile played around my lips as I remembered everything Tiy had said to me. "No," I said, "I'm sure she wouldn't mind. After all, it would be a way of remembering her, wouldn't it?"

Feeling ready to go home, I said goodbye to George and the others before heading back into the desert with Plato.

"Pleasure to have made your acquaintance!" George shouted as he waved me off.

One press of my thumb against the activation pad and Morph fired up – Plato and I climbed in. I was planning to take the time machine back to the prehistoric jungle to rescue my parents. But Morph had other ideas and, before I had a chance to do anything, the word 'home' popped up on the computer screen and we began to whizz forwards in time.

In next to no time, we had landed in Grandpa's back garden. The time machine door flew open and Plato bolted out like lightning.

I couldn't wait to go into the house to tell Grandpa about my adventure (although I'd already decided to leave out the bit about Plato dying). But I was scared that as soon as I left the time machine it would shut down and never work again. It was my only link to Mum and Dad, the only real shot I had at getting them back. If I could just have a few hours, maybe I could find a way to get the time machine to take me back to where I wanted to go – the prehistoric jungle – rather than wherever it wanted to go.

"Time to come out now," I heard Grandpa say softly from outside.

"Er, I think I might just hang out here a while, Grandpa," I said in a shaky voice. I wanted to be happy. Yes, I'd been on another good Adventure and, yes, I'd lifted an ancient curse and brought Plato back from the dead, but all I could think about was Mum and Dad.

Then a thought struck me. "Grandpa!" I said, flinging open Morph's door. "Do you think my special Adventuring skill could be time travelling?" I asked with excitement, remembering what George had said.

Grandpa blinked several times and then spoke.

"Have you tried sailing around the world on a matchstick raft?" he asked.

"Er...no."

"What about speaking Japanese?"

"No," I said.

*crypto-
WHAT?!*

"How about crypto-zoology? Or piloting planes? Driving invisible cars?"

I shook my head. Grandpa chuckled and walked towards the house. "Until you've tried a few more things," he called behind him, "I think you'll have to wait to find out what your special skill is."

I was trying to imagine what it would be like to drive an invisible car as I stepped out of Morph. Morph made a familiar clunking noise as it shut down, and I turned around to see it shrink back down into a mini time machine and spit out the time machine chip.

The area of grass the time machine had landed

on had been completely flattened. In the middle was a white envelope with my name on it.

I picked up Morph and put the mini time machine in my pocket, then ripped open the envelope…

WHAT KIND OF BOY DOES A MUMMY TAKE ON A DATE? ANY OLD BOY SHE CAN DIG UP!

CONGRATULATIONS!

YOU'VE LIFTED AN ANCIENT CURSE AND SOLVED ANOTHER MYSTERY. YOU'VE DONE YOUR FAMILY PROUD, WILL. IT LOOKS AS THOUGH YOU'RE GOING TO GROW UP TO BE A VERY POWERFUL ADVENTURER. GIVE IT SOME TIME, THEN TRY TO USE THE TIME MACHINE AGAIN.

P.S. THIS WON'T BE YOUR LAST ENCOUNTER WITH TIME TRAVEL.

CHAPTER ELEVEN
THE BRITISH MUSEUM

Grandpa was on the phone when I came into the kitchen. Half-listening to his conversation, I made myself a chocolate sandwich. ← *Yum!*

"Of course, Mrs Simmons...I understand."

My heart lurched as Grandpa put down the phone.

"I was just talking to your teacher," he said. "She wanted to make sure you had been working hard on your summer project."

"I have the whole summer to work on my project, Grandpa," I said, rolling my eyes.

"The whole summer has been and gone, boy," he said. "You were gone for five weeks."

"Impossible!" I shrieked, spitting sandwich

everywhere. "I was gone one day – max."

"The time machine has obviously brought you too far into the future," he said. "I wouldn't waste time going back and forth now. I'll take you to the City Museum tomorrow to look at the treasures of Queen Tiy's tomb. An ancestor of yours excavated them about eighty years ago. I thought they would make an excellent subject for your Egyptian project."

At no point did I tell Grandpa the details of my Adventure. So how he knew anything about Queen Tiy or George was anyone's guess.

I knew Grandpa Monty well enough to know that there was no point asking him any questions. He'd only give me a load of nonsense in reply, so after dinner I headed up to my room.

I turned Morph into a computer so I could go online.

An IM from Zoe popped up straight away.

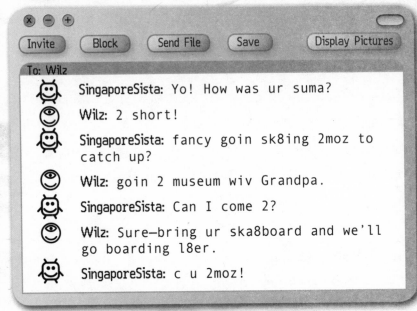

SingaporeSista: Yo! How was ur suma?

Wilz: 2 short!

SingaporeSista: fancy goin sk8ing 2moz to catch up?

Wilz: goin 2 museum wiv Grandpa.

SingaporeSista: Can I come 2?

Wilz: Sure—bring ur ska8board and we'll go boarding 18er.

SingaporeSista: c u 2moz!

Zoe came over the next day and Stanley drove me, Zoe and Grandpa to London.

Grandpa slept and snored for the whole journey while I told Zoe all about my summer fighting zombie mummies.

Grandpa knew one of the curators in the British

Museum so we had a behind-the-scenes tour. We saw the treasures that George had excavated from Queen Tiy's tomb.

Then I saw something that looked strangely familiar in one of the display cabinets. It was the other half of the lucky coin that Tiy had given me. I pulled my half out of my pocket and held it up to the glass so both halves made a whole. I gasped. When the coin halves were put together, they had an image of a Partek face on them!

"Is that what I think it is?" said Zoe.

"If it is then even the ancient Egyptians knew about them," I answered. "Come on, let's go home."

Stanley drove us home, and Zoe and I went skateboarding until dinner time. After that her

HOW?

mum came to pick her up.

Over the next couple of days I worked on my project. I used everything I'd learnt and seen during my time in ancient Egypt: the temple, Anubis, High Priests and Priestesses, mummies. It was the best project I'd ever written.

As I flipped the blankets back so I could get into bed, there was a letter waiting for me.

WHY DID THE MUMMY LEAVE HER TOMB AFTER 1000 YEARS?
BECAUSE SHE THOUGHT SHE WAS OLD ENOUGH TO LEAVE HOME!

IT'S NOT LONG BEFORE YOUR NEXT ADVENTURE. FROM NOW ON, YOU'RE GOING TO GET CLUES THAT WILL LEAD YOU TO YOUR PARENTS. THIS IS YOUR FIRST CLUE.

YOU WILL FIND ONE PARENT BEFORE YOU FIND THE OTHER.

This is driving me crazy!

What did that mean? Were my parents both alone? Had they been separated? Were they still in a prehistoric jungle or had they moved through time and got stuck somewhere else?

The letters were beginning to frustrate me more and more. They were making everything more confusing!

So what was I supposed to do now? I knew exactly what I was going to do – I was going to fire up that time machine again and search every period of history until I got Mum and Dad back, and I was going to have loads of fun on the way.

OTHER BOOKS IN THE SERIES